This Book Belongs to: _____
Given on this ____ day in the month of _____
in the year _____ Given by: _____

WestBow Press books may be ordered through booksellers or by contacting:

WestBow Press
A Division of Thomas Nelson & Zondervan
1663 Liberty Drive
Bloomington, IN 47403
www.westbowpress.com
1 (866) 928-1240

All illustrations and interior images by the author. Mr. Fredrick Gonzales MS.Ed

ISBN: 978-1-9736-9092-4 (sc)
ISBN: 978-1-9736-9107-5 (e)

Library of Congress Control Number: 2020907724

Print information available on the last page.

WestBow Press rev. date: 5/29/2020

WESTBOW
PRESS®
A DIVISION OF THOMAS NELSON
& ZONDERVAN

Freddy from the Pond in: The Bully Frogs

The Adventures of Freddy from the Pond - Book II

Written & Illustrated by Fredrick Gonzales MS.Ed

One fine day Freddy the Frog was hopping his way to school as he was singing his favorite song called "Ribbit Ribbit" and it goes like this!

All the little frogs go

Ribbit Ribbit!

When they're sitting on a log they go

Ribbit Ribbit!

Now everybody sing along

Ribbit Ribbit!

You can't go wrong just

Ribbit Ribbit!

The name of the song is

Ribbit Ribbit!

When all of a sudden, his face ran into what felt like a BIG, GIANT MARSHMALLOW!

He went, "Ribbit Rib-Ahhhhh!"

POOMPF!!!!

But it wasn't a BIG, GIANT Marshmallow,

It was the BELLY of BIG, GIANT BULLFROG!

His froggy face hit so hard that Freddy left his face print right on the bullfrog's shirt!

"Hi, I'm Freddy from the Pond.

What's your name?" asked
Freddy in a very timid voice.

"My name is Maurice. This is Clyde. And
That's Matilda, and we're Bullfrogs!"

"Well, it's mighty fine to meet you! I'm on my way to school; we're going to the museum today."

"Hey Maurice, what's a museum?" asked Clyde. Maurice answered, "It's a big fancy building with lots of fancy pictures."

You're welcome to come -
said Freddy nervously.

It's got lots of famous paintings like;

"The Girly Frog with the Pearl Earring"

"The Water Lily Frog" and the
most famous painting of all,

"The Froggy Lisa" by Leofroggo Da Vinci.

"Well, guess what little froggy? We don't like museums with all those fancy, wancy paintings by fancy, wancy artists!!!"

"How about you give us your lunch and your money instead?" croaked Matilda.

"Geez... Well, my mom packed my lunch, and she only gave me enough money to buy a souvenir at the museum."

"That'll do just fine!" growled Maurice.
They all laughed as they hopped away
with Freddy's lunch and souvenir money.

When Freddy came home after his field trip, he was sad.

"What's wrong?" asked his mom.

"Some bully frogs took my lunch and my souvenir money."

"Aw, are you okay darling?"

asked his mom lovingly.

I'm okay, but I'm worried about the bully frogs, they don't have anyone to pack them a lunch or give them lunch money.

Well tomorrow morning I can help you pack 3 extra lunches.

"Wow! That would be totally awesome!" croaked Freddy.

The next day Freddy hopped into the bully frogs again, this time Freddy was prepared.

Before you take my lunch, I brought lunch for all of us croaked Freddy.

But it was the same old story and they took his lunch anyway. This time when they hopped away, something fell out of Maurice's pocket!

It was a picture of a hairy spider!

It said;

"Lost tarantula - Please help! Answers to Fangelo"

Fangelo had a special mark
right on his back,

And it looked just like a question mark "?"

And that day when hopping home guess who Freddy found?

Yup, it was Fangelo and you could tell it was him because he had that question mark right on his back.

The next day right when they were going to take Freddy's lunch, Freddy pulled out Fangelo.

Maurice was shocked and he started to get tears in his eyes!

FANGELO!!!

Yelled Maurice!

And right there and then he started to hug Freddy.

And he thanked him over and over.

Then out of nowhere, Maurice said,
"You are now a friend of the Bull frogs,
and we will always protect you!"

Later Freddy's mom said that he did a very nice thing, but sometimes bullies don't change until grown-ups get involved,

And if it ever happens again to make sure to tell her or an adult he can trust;

Like a teacher or a principal.
It can happen, just saying.

The End